MW01675310

introduced to LOVE

Jeanette Barron

JEANETTE BARRON

introduced to LOVE

a novel

Tate Publishing & *Enterprises*

Introduced to Love
Copyright © 2010 by Jeanette Barron. All rights reserved.

No part of this publication may be reproduced, stored in a retrieval system or transmitted in any way by any means, electronic, mechanical, photocopy, recording or otherwise without the prior permission of the author except as provided by USA copyright law.

Scriptures taken from the *Holy Bible, New International Version®*, NIV®. Copyright © 1973, 1978, 1984 by Biblica, Inc.™ Used by permission of Zondervan. All rights reserved worldwide. www.zondervan.com

This novel is a work of fiction. Names, descriptions, entities, and incidents included in the story are products of the author's imagination. Any resemblance to actual persons, events, and entities is entirely coincidental.

The opinions expressed by the author are not necessarily those of Tate Publishing, LLC.

Published by Tate Publishing & Enterprises, LLC
127 E. Trade Center Terrace | Mustang, Oklahoma 73064 USA
1.888.361.9473 | www.tatepublishing.com

Tate Publishing is committed to excellence in the publishing industry. The company reflects the philosophy established by the founders, based on Psalm 68:11,
"The Lord gave the word and great was the company of those who published it."

Book design copyright © 2010 by Tate Publishing, LLC. All rights reserved.
Cover design by Lauran Levy
Interior design by Nathan Harmony

Published in the United States of America

ISBN: 978-1-61739-299-3
1. Fiction: Christian: Romance
2. Fiction: Romance: Contemporary
10.09.28

Preface

Since the time of Adam and Eve, mankind has sinned. The result of our sin is separation from our Creator, God. He is a Father to us all and longs to redeem us; that is why Jesus Christ gave his life on the cross and shed his blood as a covering for our sin. Jesus Christ rose from the dead and now sits on the right hand of his Father in heaven.

This story is about sin and redemption. It is about longing to know our roots and where we came from. It is a love story of people who are willing to set themselves aside and give and receive forgiveness. It is about truth. It is about family.

Chapter One

He stood looking at the grave, never knowing his heart could hurt so much. How can I live without her? She was gone. He had visited her grave almost every day since. Now it was raining, but Mark didn't care. He knelt down on the closest place he could be near her. He didn't want to leave; he just wanted to die with her. When grief had its way, exhausted and empty, he knew he had to go home. Forcing himself to get up from the wet ground, he trudged to his car and drove through the gate of the cemetery. It always seemed strange to be going home without her. As he drove, he was hoping it wouldn't be long before he would join her in death. "Let it be soon," he whispered. He had never thought he could love so deeply. Women had been pleasurable interludes for him. He appreciated them but had never entertained the idea of marriage until he met Rose. He felt like he was still holding her at night, felt her near him, and found himself listening for her voice, her laughter. He sometimes called out her name in his sleep. Time had passed, and the pain dulled a little, but he knew he had forever lost the most precious thing he had known.

Mark had been given that first week off from his teaching job for bereavement. Somehow, he had pulled himself together enough to finish the school year. There had been only two months left to go. His demeanor had changed, and his students were wary of their teacher, seeing the sadness that was always with him and not knowing what to do to help him. Mark was an English teacher at the local high school. He had always loved words and had written lovely poems for Rose that delighted her when he recited them. She, in turn, had been an artist and filled their home with her paintings. He had taken pleasure in finding just the right place to hang them. She had brought beauty into their home. They had been very happy together as companions and lovers. Their passion, in both directions, seemed to almost overwhelm them. It had been good to share their love for poetry and paintings, as well as the beautiful garden they had planted together, carefully selecting the flowers that they loved the most and delighting in the beauty and sweet aroma that floated up to them as they walked hand-in-hand among the flowering plants. Roses, of course, to celebrate his Rose, filled much of the garden. The paths were laid out in such a way that as you walked by the roses, you could enjoy their sweet perfume. Mark missed her so much; the pain was almost more than he could bear, but somehow, the months had passed. It was summer now, and the garden was in full bloom, reminding him of Rose and the love they shared.

Arriving home, he went to the kitchen and made a cup of tea to warm him up. He was still damp, but he didn't care. Standing at the window, he looked out while he drank his tea. His heart still mourned, and he knew it always would, but he had managed to carry on. *What is the point of it all?* "I may be alive, but it feels like I'm dead on the inside." He remembered how much she had loved this place and the dreams they had shared. He didn't want to see those dreams filled without her. Selling the place was an option he had thought about, but how could he when he still felt her presence? He saw her in every room, remembered her sitting in the rocking chair, fixing dinner, picking roses from the garden. Besides, the farm had been in the family for three generations. "Did that really matter?" Somehow, he knew it did.

He thought about his grandfather, John Sterling, who had been born in 1897. He had bought the land, developed the farm, built the barn, and loved it all. His grandmother had taken delight in country living. She minded the chickens and sold fresh eggs to the town market. Keeping a kitchen garden was also her domain, yielding tender lettuce for salads and all sorts of vegetables for their dinner table. She also put up preserves each year. They were both hard workers and did well on the farm they loved. They had been blessed with one son, Mark's father, James. Grandpa raised James to be a farmer also. James took to the land just as his dad before him had. He loved the rich earth and the smell of newly mown hay. He had planted more fruit trees and the raspberry bushes that gave them such delicious jelly. Grandpa had fought with the army forces in the First World War. Coming home, he worked hard to keep the farm going. James had been born in 1933 when Grandpa was thirty-six and thought there would be no child for them. Then James had taken over the farm after Grandpa passed away at age sixty-two in 1959, and Grandma, Betty Sterling, followed him in 1960. James had gone to Korea in 1951 in what was officially not called a war, but it sure felt like one to him. He returned home, and in 1963 had married Mary Peterson, who came from a farming background and had loved the place almost as much as James had. They were delighted when Mark was born in 1965. Mark grew into a handsome and strong young man. The days outside working the farm with his dad put color in his skin and muscles on his body. He did well in school and got good grades, which made his parents proud of him. Great sadness came to him when Mark's parents had died together in an automobile accident in 1983, just after Mark had graduated from high school. Mark had taken a year off before joining the navy, where he had been shipped overseas for a two-year tour of duty. Returning home in 1986, he farmed the property and attended college, where he got his degree to teach English. Mark felt like his life was finally together, and his thoughts turned to the idea of someday marrying and having a son to carry on the farm after him, but it would never happen now that Rose was gone. He felt that he would surely be the end of the farm and the family.

Entering the kitchen, Mark saw the teapot shaped like a rabbit and remembered how delighted Rose had been when they found it the flea market. Rose had laughed to see the bunny rabbits playing on their lawn and fell in love with the teapot immediately, so Mark had purchased it for her, hiding it behind his back while she danced around him and finally paid a kiss for it. They had loved going to the flea markets and looking over all the antiques and the stuff called "antiques" that were really just old and no longer of any use. He could move the teapot, pack it away, or give it away, but no, this was the place Rose had kept it. So many things reminded him of her. It was torture and a comfort at the same time. He knew he had to shake himself out of this and move on with life. He just didn't know why or how, or, for that matter, if he even wanted to.

Jane had been searching for weeks, looking for her birth mother. First, there was the trip to Chester, Vermont, where she learned Rose had been working for an art dealer, but that was years ago. Her father had told her that was all the information he knew about her mother. It had been a difficult time for them all. Paula and Dave were her step-parents and had raised Jane and loved her dearly. It was only recently after Jane had married and was pregnant with her first baby that Dave told Paula it was only right that Jane knew about her birth mother. Paula wasn't happy when Jane said she needed to meet Rose and get to know her and find out why she had abandoned her with Paula. Paula had tried to talk Jane into waiting until after her baby had been born, but Jane felt an urgency to find Rose quickly. Jane was expecting her and Matt's first child.

Rose had left for Chester, Vermont, and it had been almost impossible to trace her. It had been a blessing when someone mentioned she try Birmingham. In the library there, Jane had found the public records listing Rose Merryweather in the 1990 census. It gave an address and town. Jane had gone there. At the address, the people had remembered Rose. It was a while ago, but they had moved into the apartment after Rose when she left to marry. They had met Rose, and she had been so happy and in love, and it made an impression on them. They couldn't remember his name but suggested Jane check out art galleries, as Rose had been an art dealer. She might have continued working. Jane had followed up that suggestion and contacted every gallery she could find. At last, she hit pay dirt. One gallery not only remembered Rose but gave Jane the name of the man she had married. It was a Mr. Mark Sterling, who lived in Stokey, Vermont. With a prayer of thankfulness to God for showing her the path to finding her birth mother, she headed there. That was where Jane had gone, and driving through the town, Jane saw an art gallery and knew she was at last in the right place. She had checked into the local motel and looked up the name in the phone book. Mark Sterling was still listed. Getting directions from the desk clerk, she decided to visit her right away.

Jane was very nervous as she drove to find her mother. There was a feeling of foreboding. That sense of foreboding was still with her when she arrived, and she wondered how she would be received. How would Rose respond to seeing her?

She had heard of people who refused to even speak to a child of theirs they had given away and were very upset with them for trying to find them. She prayed a quiet prayer that this would not be the case with her. She had also heard of people finding their mothers and wishing they hadn't. It had turned out they were not at all what they had hoped for or expected. She believed in God's leading and protection over her. She knew there were no mistakes or accidents. She believed that God alone was the creator of life, that God, for his own reasons, placed a baby where he wanted the baby to be born and to whom. She believed in his purpose and plan. Some might say to her, "Then why not just be happy and satisfied with where you are? Why look for another mother just because she bore you, when you've got a mother who has loved and raised you all your life? Isn't that the result of God placing you there?" Jane was confused by questions; all this was thought provoking, but it doesn't answer the emotions she was feeling. There was a longing in her she couldn't explain. She needed to be anchored. She loved her Father God and considered herself to be faithful, but he was invisible, and she couldn't see him. She knew that Jesus was the Savior, but she couldn't see him either. It was like knowing about someone but never really seeing them. That was how it was with her birth mother, knowing about her but never seeing her. It left her feeling lost somehow.

The doorbell was ringing, intruding on his thoughts. *I don't want company.* He looked out the window. A stranger was standing there. "Go away!" he yelled. "Leave me alone, *probably a silly woman selling Avon.* Ignoring the ringing he walked away. It kept ringing. *What is her problem?* "Go away!" he yelled again. The bell rang, and in exasperation, he flung open the door. For a moment he thought she had come back to him. He froze and stared. When his heart recovered from the shock, he realized there was a slight difference. Her eyes were blue, not green, and her hair was red but different. Her nose was slightly crooked.

Holding tightly to self-control, he said, "Who are you?"

"I am looking for Rose Merryweather," the girl replied. "Is she here?"

Merryweather, he thought. *Why, that was Rose's maiden name.* "No," he replied. "You're too late. She died months ago."

The girl burst into tears. "Oh no," she said, crying. "I've come too late. I'm Jane Nicolson, Rose's daughter."

"Well, I'm Rose's husband, and she had no daughter." Mark was angry. How dare she say she was Rose's daughter? "I don't know what you're trying to pull, but you had better get out of here before I call the police." Mark slammed the door.

Jane stood, unable to move; shock and grief filled her. *This was the man my mother married?* "Oh, God," Jane said, crying. "Help me."

Jane had looked like Rose. Could it be? *No way,* he thought. He peeked out the window, she was still there.

What should I do? She's standing in the rain, crying. Why doesn't she just go away? It's not my fault she made a mistake. Why does she think Rose was her mother? I'll give her a cup of tea and ask her and then send her packing. He opened the door. "Come in. Standing in the rain, crying, you look like a drowned puppy. You could probably use a cup of tea."

Mark led Jane to the kitchen but couldn't bring himself to use Rose's teapot. Instead, he put the kettle on and reached for two mugs and the teabags. *No loose tea and brewing for this girl.*

"Have a seat at the table. This will just take a few moments," Mark said as he handed her a box of tissues. Jane obeyed and sat down.

Jane was studying Mr. Sterling as he made the tea. She thought him good-looking, with brown hair, maybe six feet tall, and of medium build, even though his arms suggested he was a man used to physical labor. Mark had been stalling for time to think as he made the tea. He felt confused; she certainly looked innocent enough. He was more determined than ever to get to the bottom of this.

Mark joined Jane at the table. "Okay, young lady, what is this all about?"

"Mr. Sterling—," Jane began.

He interrupted, "My name is Mark," he said, Jane smiled and began again.

"Mark, I've been tracing my birth mother for some time. I was adopted by a wonderful family, whom I love very much."

"Why aren't you satisfied with them, he asked?"

"I have this need to know why I was given up. I had no intention of intruding on Rose or her family in any way—"

"But you have," he said. "You are intruding on me."

"I just wanted to talk with her. I am deeply sorry for your loss and mine."

"You can't lose what you've never had. I'm the one who has lost someone," he said.

"Mark I am twenty-four years old and have never known her, and now I never will. Your pain must be almost unbearable, and I do not want to cause you any more pain.

"Well you certainly have given me a shock, haven't you?"

"I'm sorry. At some future time if you could find it in your heart to talk with me and tell me about Rose, I would be very grateful. I would like to know what she was like. It might help me to understand why she gave me up."

"And that's so important to you, huh? A mother must be in a very painful situation to give away her baby. What makes you think she didn't do it willingly? Not all women want to be mothers, you know."

"I'm married to a wonderful man named Matthew Nicolson. We're having our first baby in six months. I have a wonderful mother and father back home."

"But you're here looking for a mother?"

"I love them very much, but I have this sense of a hole in my heart where my birth mother should be. I don't pretend to understand, but I have this loss of identity thing going on."

"I don't see how I can help you," he said.

"My Dad had no information for me except the name Rose Merryweather and that she went to Vermont, so I came here looking for her. Here is my driver's license. I am writing down my home address and my phone number. I'm at the Holiday Inn in town, if you can find it in your heart to talk with me, please call. Thank you for giving me tea."

Getting up she said, I'll go now and hope to hear from you."

Mark escorted her to the door. "You're welcome for the tea," he said, "and we'll see, after I've given this matter some thought. You took me by surprise and gave me quite a shock. Rose had never mentioned a child."

Muttering to herself she said, "At least he didn't shut the door in my face again, and he did give me a cup of tea." But the feeling of foreboding was still there for some reason. *I must just be tired,* she thought as she headed back to town. Had she really been afraid of him? He seemed gruff, but maybe that was just his grief and surprise at her turning up claiming to be Rose's daughter. Now that she thought about it, she must have given him a real shock. *I wonder why Rose never told him about me, was she ashamed of me or herself? Dear Lord, there is deep water here. Please help me to understand and do the right thing, and God, please keep me safe.*

Jane was glad to get back to her room at the hotel. She felt exhausted, and she needed to call Matt. It was always such a comfort to talk things over with her husband. How she wished he could be here with her now. She understood his job and all the responsibilities he carried, and he hadn't wanted her to come on her own, but she had a sense of urgency that wouldn't let go of her, so they finally agreed that she would go alone. She knew Matt was covering her in prayer. He had told her to call at the smallest problem, and he would fly out to be with her. Now she understood the urgency. Rose had been dying.

I don't understand, God. Why did you bring me here too late? Have I missed what I thought you were telling me? Why didn't Dad tell me about my birth mother sooner? Did he miss what you were saying to him? God, I believe you direct our steps. Please let your peace reign in me. It is such a disappointment to find out you're adopted, search and find your birth mother, only to be told she died a few months before you got there. I need to talk with Matt. The sense of foreboding was even stronger as she dialed the phone.

Chapter Two

Mark had a lot to think about. When he and Rose had been married for a while, his thoughts had turned to the possibility of having a son. They were settling down nicely, and Mark was remembering his grandfather and his dad and their love for the farm. How he was the third generation to live and work there. It seemed only right to produce a fourth to carry on. The more he thought about it, he loved the idea of a son following him around. Mark knew Rose would be a great mother, and he would do his best for his son. That wasn't the main reason for wanting a son or, for that matter, a daughter. He loved Rose so much, and the thought of their having a child together was a longing stirring inside of him. He could picture Rose as a mother. He had broached the subject to Rose, and she agreed; a son or daughter was something she desired very much.

Another year had passed, and when there was no pregnancy, they had consulted their doctor. They had all the tests done, only to find out that Rose could never have a child. Mark had tried to reassure Rose that it didn't matter; after all, they had each other, but they both had secretly mourned for the child they would never have. Several months passed, and Rose had suggested adoption. Mark wasn't sure he wanted someone else's child. They had discussed it over and over and finally reached an agreement. They would adopt.

It had never happened. Mark's world fell apart when Rose was found to have lung cancer. They had gone through terrible days. Mark saw her suffering and tried to help her in any way he could, but all the time it was breaking his heart. It tore him apart, and just holding on was almost unbearable, but he had to keep it together for Rose. Then the end came. Hope was always with Mark until Rose passed away, and then his hope died, and he wished he could too. He had tended to her, suffered with her, and held hope up before her, but she had died. Where was her miracle? Where was God? *Strange how we go through life and never think about God until we are in a crisis situation, and then if things don't work out for us, we blame God.* Mark had not been raised in a church, but he had friends who were who had tried to tell him about God. He just had never seen a need for one. Even when his parents died, he had thought of God, if he existed, as the reason for their death. Rose was not a church person either, and they had never talked about the possibility of a God until she became ill.

Mark didn't believe in this God. He felt God had failed him. Mark had told her so many times to stop smoking, but it was an addiction with Rose, a craving she couldn't seem to overcome, and it had killed her. Since her death, he seemed to be walking in a daze, hating everything and everyone. He was convinced that there was no God. If there were, why would he let this happen?

Now this woman claims Rose was her mother. Mark knew it was not possible. What was Jane pulling and why? What could she benefit from claiming this birth relationship with Rose? What could be gained by this ruse? Could it be Jane actually believed Rose was her mother? Who had told her that and why? Anger rose in Mark. *How dare she, come out of the woodwork like some worm after Rose was gone and couldn't refute this woman's accusations?* Well, he could answer for Rose. He and Rose never had secrets from each other, and besides, he was part of the testing procedure and knew Rose had never had and never would have a baby. Just what was she after with her lies? Jane said she was married and three months pregnant. She had a trim shape. Was she really pregnant? If he talked with her, perhaps he could learn what was behind all this. Rose was gone, so she couldn't be hurt anymore. Could he talk about her? It would be difficult, and yet, to share about Rose would bring her closer. But what harm could this girl do? Was she after a legacy? No, there wasn't any money, just the farm, and that was his. Proving a blood relation to Rose wouldn't help anyone get an inheritance. *I just can't figure this out,* thought Mark. *Could Jane really be telling me what she thinks is the truth? Is it possible Jane's father really thinks Rose was Jane's true birth mother? Makes you wonder where he got the name from and if he knew Rose sometime in her college days. He must know then that Rose was never pregnant.*

Mark realized he would never know unless he talked with Jane. "I'll call her, but first, I'll call information and find out if Matt Nicolson is listed at the address and number she gave me. There is something very wrong here, and I am going to get to the bottom of it, but until I know what she is up to, I'll play it close to my chest. When she's comfortable, maybe she'll slip, and then I'll get her. Rose," he said as he sighed, "I wish you were here. I miss you so and sure would like to talk things over with you."

Just what do I really know about Rose he thought. *Let me see, I know she went to art school and came to Vermont when she received a job offer at a gallery in Chester. Rose was a talented artist herself. I know her parents were dead, and she had no siblings. There is a similarity in appearance—not the same—but there is something there.* "Oh, Mark," he said to himself, "cut it out. It's impossible, so don't even let yourself begin to see any similarity. You've got to keep your mind clear and not let emotions get to you."

It had been a long day, and he decided to make it an early night. Maybe a good night's sleep would lift this feeling of—what was it—anxiety and foreboding? He did not sleep well, however, tossing and turning while dreaming of being on a ship. Water was dark and seething all around him.

He awoke early and made his way to the kitchen. It was now July, and he was spending a lot of time in the gardens. Rose had loved the flowers. He was keeping the gardens weeded for her. The morning gave him the exercise and fresh air he needed to overcome the headache and prepare for Jane, now to make the phone calls.

The first call assured him that Matthew Nicolson did live at the address Jane had given him. The second call invited her to visit the next afternoon, which she eagerly accepted. *Well,* Mark thought, *no going back. I'll talk about Rose and see if she tries to make out a similarity between them. As Jane wasn't raised by Rose, she shouldn't know Rose's likes and dislikes. This should prove interesting,* thought Mark. *I wonder how much research she has done on Rose and why?*

Jane had been praying, asking God to have Mark call her. She could feel anxiety growing and took some deep breaths, trying to stay calm. "Oh, God, please—," she began, and the phone rang.

"Hello? Yes, this is Jane."

"Hello, Jane, this is Mark. I have decided to talk with you about Rose. Would you be able to visit me tomorrow, say about two in the afternoon?"

"Thank you, Mark. I'll be there." Hanging up the phone she prayed, "Oh, God, thank you for helping me. Please let all go well. Bless Mark and help him share about Rose. I know it will be painful for him, but I need to learn about my mother."

Dialing her home number and hearing Matt's voice, she blurted out, "Matt, Rose is dead. I came too late, but the man she married asked me to come by tomorrow and he'll talk with me."

"Honey, you must feel terrible," he said. "I'm so sorry."

"Say a prayer for me, Matt. I'm not sure I like this man."

"Please be careful. You don't have to do this you know. You've got me and the baby and a great mom already."

"I know, but I need to do this. I'll call when I know something more."

"Make sure you do. I'll be waiting. Love you."

"I love you too, sweetheart. Bye for now."

Jane decided to visit the library in town and get a book to read to pass the evening. She found one on the history of Stokey, Vermont and spent the evening studying it. It had started as a farm community, and industry had moved in when the paper mill was built. It had continued to grow, and there was a theater group that put on plays, an art center, and four churches of differing denominations. Jane had decided to visit them all. She liked the looks of this place. It was nice to think of Rose living here. Jane wondered if Rose belonged to any of the churches. She wondered what Mark did for a living. She would have to ask him tomorrow. There were so many questions she would like to ask.

It was just about ten in the morning, and she still had four hours before she would see Mark, so she decided a walk would be good for her. Jane found a store that sold yarn and happily bought baby blue yarn to knit a sweater for her and Matt's son; of course, she had no idea if the baby was a boy, but she hoped so. She thought the first child should be a boy; then he could be a big brother to his sister when she came. She had no sister or brother and had always wanted one or more. Jane's heart swelled within her as she whispered a thank you to God for the baby growing inside her and asked his continued care over the babe. Her mother taught her to knit and she really enjoyed the sense of fulfillment that came from hand-making something. She would make a blanket to go with the sweater when she had finished it.

She got a good start on the sweater when lunchtime came. She tucked the knitting in a tote and took it with her. She enjoyed a garden salad for lunch at a diner down the street and then happily set out for Mark's farm. She was singing and very happy, but as she neared Mark's farm, her spirits started to fall, and the singing stopped. Jane pulled into the driveway, and again, that feeling of foreboding settled on her. *What is wrong,* she wondered. *Maybe I am a little afraid of Mark. Lord, please protect me from all harm. I believe you want me to know about my birth mother. I trust you, Lord.* Taking a deep breath and swallowing the fear, Jane got out and walked to Mark's door.

Chapter Three

Mark had spent the morning in the garden thinking of Rose and wondering how he would handle the meeting with Jane. He decided there were two questions he would ask before he told her anything. One, how had she learned that Rose was her mother, and two, what about her father? He made some iced tea to serve and decided that, with the air conditioning, they would have their meeting inside today. July could be very hot in Vermont, and Jane had claimed to be pregnant, although Mark wasn't so sure about that.

Right on time, Jane pulled into Mark's driveway and parked. He watched her walk up to the door, and taking a deep breath, opened it. "Hi," he said.

Feeling a bit nervous, she said, "Hello there. Thanks for letting me come." Mark led her to the living room and got the iced tea for them.

"You have air conditioning, don't you? It feels very comfortable in here. Thank you for the tea."

Mark settled in his favorite easy chair while Jane sat on the rocker, the one that Rose had always used. She looked somewhat like Rose, and seeing her there gave Mark a funny feeling. He took a sip of his tea and decided he would start the conversation.

"Jane, I am curious. Could you tell me how you knew about Rose?"

My father told me. He said he and Mom loved me with all their hearts, but he thought it only right that I should know the truth. He said my birth mother's name was Rose Merryweather and that she was not married when she had me and couldn't take care of a baby. She left me behind and went to Chester Vermont.

"Your parents never looked for her or tried to find her?"

"No, they accepted me as theirs, I guess, and never thought anymore about it. I have no brothers or sisters, I'm their only child."

"What about your father? Do you know who he is?"

"Of course, his name is David Carlin."

"So your father and Rose weren't married?"

Jane looked surprised. "My father, married to Rose? He never knew Rose." Jane looked stunned. "Oh my father, Mark, I have been so busy thinking of Rose I have never given any thought to my father." Tears welled up in her eyes and slowly sled down her checks. She was devastated. How could she never think of her father? The realization that she didn't know her blood parents father or mother, washed over her. Her father had only mentioned her mother. *Does he know who my father is?* She wondered.

Mark wasn't sure what to do, so he set some tissues beside her and just waited. He was thinking to himself that this had to be real, or she was one good actress to be able to cry at will. So his theory of her father knowing Rose might be wrong.

"I'm sorry. I know it appears impossible, but I honestly never thought of my father."

Mark thought this was a bit odd.

"Thank you for the tissues," she said as she wiped her face.

Mark was thinking to himself, *her father told her about Rose but never mentioned who her real father was.* He wanted to think that David, perhaps, was the father and had known Rose very well, but no, that couldn't be, as Rose could not have a baby and was not Jane's mother. None of this was making any sense. Anger rose up inside him. He needed to cool down if he was going to get to the bottom of this farce.

"How about some more tea," he asked as he went to the kitchen taking some deep breaths. When he returned, Jane was smiling.

"Thank you," she said. "I've been wondering how you met my mother. All I know is she was in Chester and supposedly worked as an art dealer. I confess to knowing nothing about what an art dealer does, but I imagine it means she sold paintings. I do know she worked in art galleries. Do you also work as an art dealer?"

"No, I'm an English teacher. After I mustered out of the navy, I came back to the farm. I'm the third generation here now. I finished my education on the GI Bill. With a degree under my belt, I obtained a position at our local high school. Meeting Rose was the high point of my life. I never thought I would get married. I was happy just as I was, what with the farm. You see my parents were dead, and my grandparents started the farm. I was happy. I guess you could say, set in my ways. I had my teaching, which I loved, and the farm, which gave me plenty of exercise. I grew my own vegetables, and I keep a flower garden. If I needed female companionship, I had a few lady friends I dated. I had updated a room in the house. It needed one more touch to be finished—a painting for the wall. I like paintings and often visited art galleries when there was a showing of a local artist. That's why I went to Birmingham."

He had a wistful look on his face as he continued. "The place had a few people in it, and as I glanced around, a woman talking with a man across the room caught my eye. She had hair like polished, rich chestnuts, and she laughed with a lovely sound. I slowly made my way around the room, looking at the paintings but keeping my eye on her. At last, I was next to her. I pretended to concentrate on the painting before me. Soon, the man she was talking to left, and she turned to me. She stood silently for a couple minutes and then said, 'So, do you like this painting?' Smiling at her, I said, 'No, not really.' She laughed, and we got into a discussion about the artist and what he was trying to express in the painting. Her eyes were the most beautiful green I had ever seen. I was captivated. I introduced myself, and she told me she was Rose Merryweather. She asked me if I was in the market for a painting, and I told her about the room I had updated. Rose was a success as dealer of paintings because she had the ability to know just what the buyer needed. She seemed to lead them to just the right painting. After asking me a few questions about the room, she showed me the perfect painting, and I bought it. Come on, I'll show it to you."

Mark led her to a back room in the house and opened the door. It was lovely—all sunshine yellow and soft green. There was an old-fashioned quilt on the bed, a braided rug on the floor, and the painting. He had hung it on the wall across from the bed, so you could lie down and look at it. It was of a field of wildflowers, green grass, and yellow buttercups and dandelions—some puffy and white—ready to let their seeds go on the wind. The sky filled with big, fluffy clouds.

"Oh, I like it, Mark. What a beautiful room and the perfect painting for it."

"Rose really had an expertise in paintings," he told her as they returned to the living room. "I've never been shy when it comes to women, and this was one I really wanted to get to know. I was, for the first time in my life, feeling flustered. She packed up the painting for me, I paid, and she moved on to talk with another patron. I left, wondering why I hadn't asked her out. I have never been so tongue-tied. I drove home in a fog. I decided I would return the next Saturday and take her to lunch, and I did just that. I timed my arrival for lunchtime, and she didn't seem the least surprised to see me. However, she couldn't leave, as she was alone covering the gallery while the boss took care of some business, and the gallery was busy. We arranged for me to pick her up at the gallery the next Saturday and go for dinner. I scouted the town, found a nice restaurant, and had lunch there to make sure it was good and went home whistling.

"The week seemed to drag. I was almost beside myself waiting for Saturday to come. It did, and off I went to dinner with my Rose. She was ready when I got there and delighted with the restaurant I had selected. She had eaten there before and liked it very much. She had a green dress on that made her eyes sparkle, or maybe it was her eyes that made the dress look so pretty. Little dangling earrings with green glass bobbles hung from her ears. She smelled like roses, and I knew I was in love already."

"Oh, how romantic, she sounds beautiful."

"She was," he said. "And that's enough if you'll excuse me."

She could see the pain in his eyes and felt guilty for putting him through this memory. "Of course," she said.

He led her to the door. "Tomorrow Same time," he said and shut her out.

As she drove back to the hotel, she now understood that Mark's gruff manner was his pain showing though. She knew this was hurting him and had a sense of guilt for causing him to remember. But she so wanted to know about Rose.

Arriving in her room, she laid down on the bed for a rest to think over what she had learned. After a good rest, shc pickcd up thc phonc to call Matt.

After hearing about all she had learned, he said, "Sure, I'll talk to your dad and see if he knows anything about your birth father. I think it's a bit strange that no one ever mentioned him, don't you?

"Well it seems strange to me that's for sure. You know honey Mark made my mother sound so beautiful. They really were in love."

"Just like us," he said.

"I'll be waiting to hear from you, bye for now darling."

Jane was still tired even though she had rested, she got ready for bed. She supposed it was the emotions of the day, and the fact that the baby needed sleep. She drifted off, dreaming of a green-eyed woman with chestnut hair—her mother.

Chapter Four

Jane heard from Matt first thing in the morning. "I've spoken with your dad. He knew nothing about who your birth father might be. He asked your mother, and she didn't know either."

"I don't understand, honey. It seems like my birth is some big mystery. Wouldn't my mother have told mom who my father was?"

"I admit it seems odd, but we'll find out, maybe Mark will be able to tell you more."

"I'll call you later, honey. I miss you and I love you."

"Bye for now."

Jane was anxious to see Mark and learn more about Rose, and he was waiting for her. The door was open, and Mark called, "Come on in, Jane. Hi there. So how are you today? You look rested."

"I am, and you?"

"Fine," he said. "Will you have iced tea, or do you prefer something else?"

"No, tea will be fine. Thanks." She went into the living room and sat in the rocker. Such a comfortable house this was.

"Here's your iced tea," he said as he sat down in his favorite chair. "What is that you have with you?"

"My knitting, I am making a sweater for the baby, I'll make a blanket to go with it. I thought I'd work on it while we talk, that is, if you don't mind."

"I don't mind at all," said Mark. "I see you're using blue. Does that mean you know you're having a boy?"

Jane smiled. "Oh, we don't know, but I would like a boy, so I've asked God. I believe God will give us a son."

"Oh, you believe in God?"

"Yes, don't you, Mark?

"No, Jane, if there were a God, my Rose wouldn't be dead from cancer and buried. She was only forty-six, you know. We had so much living yet to do. No, I don't believe in God."

Jane didn't know what to say. She supposed she should witness to him about the truth of Jesus as Savior, but she realized he wouldn't listen, and she really didn't know what to say. "I'm sorry," was all she could think of. Here she was, happy over having a baby, and he was sitting here hurting over his loss. She realized as a non-believer, he felt hopeless. It was an awkward moment for her. She didn't know what to say, but in her heart, she was saying, *Dear God, help Mark.*

"I can in no way know the pain you're feeling, Mark. I've never lost a loved one. This may sound weird to you, but I do feel emptiness in me in a place where I should feel secure. Oh, it is so hard to describe! What are you? I mean English, German, what? You see, I have no idea what I am. I can tell from my coloring and looks that I'm Caucasian. I could guess at the root of my ancestry. I know people say they need to know their parents for medical reasons. You know, to see if there are any diseases, etc., running in the family. I know nothing. I feel loved and part of a family, but still, there is this lost feeling. I'm saying this all wrong."

"Jane, if it's one thing I do understand, it's the empty feeling of someone missing from your life. Believe me. I'll try to help you. I am the third generation on this farm. I have a sense of family and ancestry. I know my roots. I can understand your feeling of loss." *Can I ever,* he thought. *Oh, Rose.*

"I'm going to have a baby, and I want my son to know whom he is. Yes, there is his father's side, but what am I bringing to him? I'm sorry to ask, but Rose died from cancer. What kind of cancer did you say it was? Could I have it also?"

"Do you smoke, Jane?"

"No."

"Well, Rose did. It was a habit she couldn't break, and it broke her. She suffered a lot."

"I'm so sorry. Oh my, I seem to keep saying that."

"It's okay. You couldn't feel any sorrier than I do. Come with me. I want to show you something."

Mark led Jane into a room on the far side of the house. It faced the light and was windowed on one complete side and had a skylight above. A bright room full of light. Jane gasped. There was an easel with a large painting on it. It was a man and woman walking in a garden. They were smiling at each other, and you could see the love in their eyes. He was holding a red rose in his hand, and she was reaching to receive it from him. Tears came to Jane's eyes. This was her mother and Mark. She was beautiful. Mark picked up a cloth and covered the painting.

"Yes," he said. "She was very beautiful. Look here. All these paintings along the wall are Rose's. She was a great artist in her own right."

Jane was in amazement. There were several garden ones and paintings of many different flowers.

"Rose loved flowers of all sorts. She enjoyed painting them." There were also paintings of the sea with the wind whipping up the waves, one with waves crashing on the shore, spray shooting up into the air; one had a sailboat with the setting sun behind it. There were sunrises over the mountains with trees touched by the gold of the sun. Jane stood in awe.

"My mother was very talented. These paintings are wonderful. They take my breath away with their beauty. What a treasure she left behind for you."

Mark didn't answer her. *A treasure,* he thought. *Rose was my treasure. These paintings are painful reminders of my loss.* "Let us return to the living room. I don't go into her studio much. Her presence is still there, and it haunts me. Now you know a little more about my Rose."

"Thank you, for sharing her paintings with me. I feel as if she has reached out and somehow touched my soul. She certainly had an eye for beauty and color. Of course,

I knew she sold paintings and worked in art galleries. I should have realized she also was a painter."

Sitting back down in what had become her favorite chair in the living room, perhaps because it was a rocking chair, and she felt so maternal knitting there and talking about her birth mother with Mark, she said, "My husband spoke with my dad about who my birth father was. Dad said he had no idea and had asked Mom, and she said she had no idea either. Do you think he could have been an artist?"

Anger stirred in Mark. How dare she suggest Rose being with another man? Rose had been his only. She wasn't Jane's mother. Mark excused himself and went for more iced tea. He needed a chance to calm down. Didn't Jane realize that Rose's talent was hers alone and that Rose had been his alone? *Why don't I end this right now and throw her out of here,* he thought. *Rose, Rose, how dare she.* He counted to ten slowly—a habit he had learned from his mother to calm himself. He reasoned with himself. He knew he was feeling jealousy over the suggestion of another man in Rose's life. *Why does everything continue to hurt?*

When he returned to his chair, Jane was knitting. She smiled at him, and he couldn't help thinking how sweet she looked sitting there with her knitting. She really was a nice girl. She was suffering. He could understand her need to know about her birth, but somehow, she had gotten the wrong information, and he wanted to know why.

"Jane, did your father ever tell you how he got the information about Rose and your birth?"

"Well, when Dad met Mom, she already had me. So I guess from my mom. I thought she had adopted me, but you know, she might have known Rose herself and just agreed to take me as her own when Rose left for Vermont. I don't know why, but I've never talked with Mom about Rose. I guess I just didn't want to hurt her feelings. She loves me. I wouldn't want her to think I preferred a different mom."

"Jane, have you ever seen any adoption papers?"

"Why no, I haven't. I never asked. I only assumed I had been adopted."

"What if you hadn't been? You should ask your parents about that. Sometimes you can find out information, like where you were adopted from and when, by whom and from whom. Today, the records are pretty well open, you know."

"You're right. I should look into this. When I talk with Matt tonight, I'll ask him to see my folks for me and question them on adoption papers."

"Well, if you don't mind, that's enough for today. You have something to think about, and I have some work to do in the gardens, tomorrow, same time?"

"Thank you. I'll be here. You don't have to see me out. I know the way. Can I bring you anything from town?"

"No thanks. I'm fine. See you tomorrow. Bye."

Jane was confused. She drove back to the hotel in a bit of a daze. She needed to clear her head. Arriving at the hotel, she decided to take a short walk. She started to think of names for their son, and when she got back, she picked up the phone and called Matt. They had fun laughing over names like Mortimer and Sylvester, the best being Nicky Nicolson.

"Honey, will you ask Mom and Dad about adoption papers? I've never seen any or even given them a thought."

"Sure, you know you might be able to get some information from them about your birth father. I'll ask your dad and try not to upset your mom."

"Mark showed me a painting Rose did of the two of them standing in their garden, looking into each other's eyes. He said, 'I miss her so much, to see her even in a painting makes my heart leap.' How difficult it must have been for Mark to lose her. I can't imagine what I would do if anything happened to you."

Matt said, "How does one survive without knowing God?" They joined their voices in a prayer for Mark and a sense of peace flowed over them both. Their conversation had warmed her and left her longing to be in Matt's arms. How she wished he were here with her. *One more day,* she thought.

"Good night, my love, until tomorrow. I'll call again after my afternoon with Mark."

With some tender words exchanged between them, they said good night. Jane prepared for bed, and sitting against the pillows, she knitted for a while until she fell asleep, her mind on what the adoption papers might tell her and who her father was.

Chapter Five

Jane awoke, stretched, and snuggled back down. She didn't want to face this day yet. She felt odd—like something was going to happen. She could feel it in her bones. Something was not right. She felt disturbed somehow that feeling of heaviness. The words "put on the garment of praise, for the spirit of heaviness" came to her mind, and Jane began to praise God, telling him how she loved him and thanking him for his care of her and her baby. Everything had been going fairly well.

"I wonder why I am feeling this way. Dear God, please wrap your arms of protection around me and my baby," Jane prayed. She showered and dressed and decided some breakfast might make her feel better. A big glass of orange juice, liquid sunshine, would be nice.

Mark awoke with a headache. He felt grumpy and out of sorts. *I can't do this. Jane is sweet, but she is not Rose's. I've had enough.* He made his way to the kitchen and started the coffee. It was ready when he had washed and dressed.

With mug in hand, he went to the studio. *I must make peace somehow with Rose's death,* he thought. He realized he would always miss her, but he must get a grip on things. *First,* he thought, *I'll settle this matter with Jane. Somehow, she has gotten the wrong information, and she needs to know that. Rose couldn't possibly be her birth mother, as her father had told her. He thought it was only right she knew about her birth. I think he's right. It's only right that I tell her Rose is not her mother, so she can get on with finding out the truth about her birth.*

With his mind made up, he started to feel better. "Okay, Rose," he said. "This is going to be a tough day." *Breakfast,* he thought. *I'm hungry.* He seemed surprised to realize that. *Let me see, I think bacon and eggs with toast and that blueberry jam I bought last week will do the trick.* He actually did feel better. He guessed it was because he had made the decision, and this farce would be over today, one way or another.

Jane finished her breakfast and decided to return to her room. She knew Matt would be at work, but the urge to call him was overpowering. She picked up the phone and made the call.

"Jane, what's wrong? Are you all right?"

"I'm fine, Matt. I just needed to talk with you, darling. Are you busy? Can you give me a few minutes?"

"Of course I can, honey, but what is it? Are you sure you're okay?"

"Yes, baby and I are fine. Did you ask Dad about the adoption papers?"

"Yes, I did, honey, and he said he has never seen any. He asked your mom, and she said, 'Oh, they were probably around someplace,' and when she had the chance, she would see if she could find them. Your dad said your mom seemed uncomfortable, kind of edgy. She quickly changed the subject. Knowing her as well as he does, he knew something was wrong, and she was putting him off. I don't know what's going on, Jane, but I'd feel better if you were coming home. I need you to be here. Do you think you're ready to give this up and come home?"

Jane heard the tension in Matt's voice, and it met her own feeling of trepidation. "I'm ready, but there is one thing I have to do. Tell Mark thanks and goodbye."

"You be careful he said and give me a call when you're ready to leave. I'll be watching for you."

"All right, darling," I'll stay here tonight and leave after breakfast in the morning when I'm fresh after a night's sleep. I'll call before I leave. Tell Mom and Dad I'll be seeing them soon. I miss them, and give them my love. And Matt, I miss you very much and can't wait to be in your arms. Now go back to work, darling, and I'll see you soon." Knowing she would be home in another day or so made her feel so much better. She would take one more look around the town before she went for her visit with Mark.

Oh my, Jane thought. *It's Sunday. I've lost track of the days since I've been here. I need to go to church, and I had intended to visit them all.* Jane's father had always told them they had to be in church on Sunday morning; it was the proper way to live. *Which one should I go to? Does it matter? I think I'll walk around and see if there are any churches close by. The exercise will be good for baby and me.*

She hadn't gone too far down the street when she came to a church and could hear music and singing. *This sounds nice,* she thought, so she entered. It was a beautiful sanctuary but a bit different from what she was used to back home. She slipped into a seat near the back. The music washed over her and contentment settled in her. *There is peace in this place,* she thought. The baby picked that moment to move, and she felt it for the first time. The doctor said when she would start to feel the baby move it would be like butterflies in her tummy. Joy and laughter filled her and mingled with the peace she was feeling in this place. A sense of holiness washed over her, and she felt like crying, but it was a good feeling; she felt loved.

Her heart cried out, *Oh, Jesus, I love you. Bless this day and Matt and Mom and Dad and Mark. Bless and protect my baby and me. Please go before me and prepare the ground for my meeting with Mark.* She breathed deep and relaxed into the peace, feeling wrapped in arms of love. She enjoyed the rest of the service and left feeling uplifted and full. The pastor had preached a good sermon about God's love and how he loves all that he has created. There are no accidents of birth, for only God could create life. *I'm so glad I realized it was Sunday,* she thought as she returned to her room. *I'll pack all I can now and go get some lunch, then when I return from Mark's, I can have supper and get a good night's sleep and an early start tomorrow.* Jane was eager to get home.

She was feeling comfortable and at peace. It would be nice seeing Mark. She would say goodbye and return to Matt.

When she turned into Mark's driveway, the feelings of dread returned. *Why, Lord, why? What is this feeling? I like Mark. As a matter of fact, I believe we have become friends. He seems to like me too.* She sat in the car for a moment or two and then saw Mark. He was waving from the garden, and he had some flowers in his hand. She got out of the car and waved back. Smiling, she called, "Hi, Mark picking flowers?"

"I sure am. Let me see, you remind me of a sweet pink rose, so here you are," he said, walking toward the car to meet her. "A token to remember our friendship, in spite of all that may happen between us today."

"Thanks for the rose. It's beautiful." But she felt even more on edge, wondering what Mark meant by the words "in spite of what may happen today."

"Jane, we need to have a very serious conversation, but first, let's just enjoy each other's company. I've tried to share with you about Rose, but you haven't told me much about yourself or your life, and I'd like to know you better, if you don't mind. Shall we sit over here, where we can enjoy the garden while we visit?"

I'm being foolish, Jane thought. *Of course Mark wants to know about me. He was married to my mother. I wonder if I remind him of her somehow. She was much prettier than I am, but there is some resemblance, I think.*

"Well now let me see. I told you about Matt. He's the head of his own business. He's a hydraulic engineer and drills salt recovery wells. The Watkins Glen area is a salt table at the lower end of Seneca Lake. Here's a photo of Matt," she said, digging into her purse. "Handsome, don't you think?

"He looks okay. Did you know him for long before you fell in love?"

"I fell in love with him the first time I saw him, and eighteen months later, we were married."

"It's never too fast when you truly love someone," he said.

"We are about to have our son. By the way, he moved for the first time this morning, or I should say, I felt him move for the first time this morning."

"I bet that brought a smile to your face," he said.

"I realized it was Sunday, so I went to that little church by the fire station on Main Street. That's when I felt him move. It was just like butterflies. I can't wait to tell Matt."

"Matt will be sorry he wasn't with you when it happened, but there will be plenty of times yet for him to feel his son move."

"We live in the small town of Watkins Glen, New York, as I mentioned. Perhaps you've heard of it?"

"Yes as a matter of fact, I've been there."

"They hold grand prix auto races there, and it's well-known for its waterfalls and hiking glen. Dad's family was from there, and he and his brother, Lenny, have a shoe store together. Mom is from California."

"Really, I've been to California, to San Diego when I was in the navy," he said.

"Mom met Dad when he was at a convention there. Mom worked as a waitress and served him his breakfast. Dad talked her up, and they started to see each other. She had me with her then and explained how Rose had gone to Vermont and left me with her, and as she hadn't heard a word from Rose and didn't know how to reach her, she just adopted me. When Dad proposed, she said yes, and we became a family. Mom was a little afraid when she met Dad's folks, as they were strict religious people, and Mom didn't even go to church. She didn't believe in God then, but she joined the church, and they married there. We still go there, and that's where Matt and I got married. Here I am rambling on. Do you have any questions, Mark?"

"Only one," he said. "Where in California was your mom from?"

"Gee, I'm not sure. I don't think she ever said, now that you mention it."

"Don't you think that's a little strange," he said, "not to talk about your childhood or where you grew up?"

"There are no relatives on Mom's side alive. We've never been to California, and she never talks about her time there, just about meeting my dad and serving him his eggs. She says she's been serving him eggs ever since. Matt and I live about five miles from them. We see each other on Sundays, of course."

"You sound like a close family. Isn't that enough for you? What if you never find the truth about your birth parents?"

"When I've done my part, my best, then I will accept whatever God gives me. I believe he controls my future and his way will be done in my life. I believe we are to partnership with him and do the very best we can and he will direct our steps. I accept his Lordship over my life." Looking at Mark, she laughed. "Am I totally boring you?"

"No, you're not. I'm pleased to see you so confident about your future and your ability to believe. I hope you get your son. Now how about we go in and I fix us some iced tea? I'm getting really warm sitting here in the sun."

"Okay, I could use a cold drink."

Settled in the rocker again, Jane felt right at home. She wondered if it was because she felt close to her mother here, and because Mark was comfortable to be with. *Life is so strange sometimes. It can be so full and yet leave you feeling somehow sad. Why is that?* Jane wondered. *What I am feeling? I like it here, and I like Mark. I could have been very happy here with Rose, growing up with the gardens and the paintings. I imagine Mark is a great teacher and would have taught me himself at that big table. I am grateful for the home and wonderful parents I have, even if neither one is my birth parent. They have loved and cared for me. I have a wonderful family. Oh, Matt, I miss you. Mom and Dad, I feel lost confused. I want to go home.*

"Mark," Jane said, "I need to go back to my husband and my home. I will be leaving in the morning, but I want to thank you for all your kindness. I appreciate you sharing about Rose with me, but I miss my family very much."

"Of course you do, and I agree it's time for you to return home."

"Mom and Dad have been great to me. They love me with all their hearts, and I love them. I miss Matt so much. I need to go to him. I will always remember this place. It has such a peace and beauty about it. I can feel the generations of your family here filling this house and making it truly a home where love reigned for all. It warms me, and I appreciate your kindness to me. I know this has been difficult for you. I pray that God heals your heart. I am so sorry to have missed meeting Rose, but you have brought her close, and I just know the love the two of you shared was something very special. She isn't lost, you know. She is in heaven and will meet you at the door when it's your time to cross over. I believe she would want you to carry on and achieve great things with your life. In a sense, she will always be with you.

"Wait a minute. There is something we need to discuss. This is rather difficult. I have become fond of you and enjoyed our visits, but as your dad said, you have the right to know the truth about your birth, and I agree with him. One of our greatest disappointments was that we had no children. We saw a doctor and had all the testing done. The result was that Rose could never get pregnant and had never been pregnant. Rose could not possibly be your birth mother. When you showed up here, I thought you were playing some game, and I was determined to find you out and put a stop to what sham you thought you could pull. Our visits, however, have shown me that you truly believe Rose was your birth mother. I'm sorry. We were considering adoption when Rose was diagnosed with lung cancer. I know this is hard for you to take in, but it is true. It brings us, or you, to the problem of why your mother told you Rose was your birth mother. Why would she do that?

"She must have known Rose, or she wouldn't be able to give you a name or tell you she went to Vermont. Were they friends? I had never heard of you or your family before you showed up here. I don't believe Rose would have kept secrets from me, and seeing as she couldn't have a baby, did she even know what your mom was saying about her? I don't understand this, Jane. But I do know your mother has lied to you and your father. There are questions that need answers. You do need to go home and have a talk with your parents. I would be glad to help, but I believe I have already told you all I know. I wish you luck finding your answers and with your future life. I hope your baby turns out to be the boy you both want. I'll walk you to your car."

Chapter Six

Jane was numb. She could only stare at Mark, frozen by what he had said. Her mind was in a whirl, and tears edged her eyes, ready to spill. How was this possible? Why hadn't Mark said something in the very beginning? It couldn't be true he must be lying. *Why would he do this to me?* Jane thought. *I have to get out of here, away from Mark, from this pain. Is Mark crazy?*

Jane got up and ran out the door. Jumping into her car, she quickly started the motor and tore out of the driveway. She could hear Mark yelling her name. *Concentrate,* she told herself. *You must drive safely back to town. Remember the baby. Think later, just drive.* She tried to follow her own advice and keep the tears and emotions at bay for now. It took everything in her to hold it together until she was in her room at the hotel. Once there, she flung herself on the bed, and the tears came.

She cried out, "Why? Why? How could this happen? God, God, help me, I don't understand. I must get home. No, I can't drive home now. I have to calm down and get myself under control." She took a deep breath, and now she was shivering. How could Mark do this to her? She climbed in the bed and buried herself in the covers. Shivering and weeping, she finally fell asleep.

She awoke in the middle of the night with her stomach growling and realized she had not eaten since lunch yesterday. "Poor baby," she crooned as she rubbed her tummy. "Mommy will feed you soon." Remembering a candy machine in the foyer, she got a couple chocolate bars and a can of soda. Feeling better, she finished her packing and sat to think.

Mark said Rose could never have had a baby. They had all the tests done, and there was no chance she had ever conceived a baby. He thought Jane was playing some game and had led her on to see what it was. She realized that he must really believe that.

"Rose," she questioned, as if she could hear her, "was there something he didn't know? Could the inability to have a baby happen later, after you had me? Mark had said the test showed Rose had never had a baby and could never have one. Can tests prove that?" He had been so kind to her, and she really had liked him. He made Rose so very real, and Jane felt herself responding to the person Rose had been. She felt as if she was Rose's daughter, or had it only been her mind or heart playing tricks on her? Why did she need to know her anyway? Hadn't Paula been a wonderful, loving mother to her? What was this need to know in her? *Did Mom lie to me? No, that can't be. My mother has always loved me. I know that. I have everything. Why do I feel lost, Lord? Where are you, God? Did you plan this to happen to me? I don't understand why this is happening to me, God.*

For the first time, Jane began to question if God really was real. She had always believed in Jesus as Savior, as far back as she could remember. Her family had always been in church. She had been in the children's classes, and then, an adult member. Why, she and Matt were married there. *What is happening? Haven't I always done what I was supposed to?*

"Oh, dear Jesus," Jane called out. "I do believe. Please forgive me for thinking you, even for a moment, were not the Savior. I do trust you, Father God, and I will accept your will for my life. Holy Spirit of God my helper, please fill me anew with your presence and help me to do the right thing. I will now go back to sleep and be rested for my drive home." Softly singing "Jesus Loves Me, This I Know," Jane drifted off to sleep.

Jane dozed off and on and was ready when the morning came to check out and be on her way. She decided to visit the church she had been in on Sunday and sat on a bench in the churchyard, asking Jesus to restore peace to her and for his protection on the long drive home. Sitting in the sun, she found herself relaxing.

She was on the road later than she had planned, but it was worth the time spent with the Lord. She had a long ride before her. It took about six hours, with stopping for lunch on the way. She couldn't stop thinking about what Mark had said and soon found her-self in an agitated state. *Why did Rose give me to my mother? Were she and my mom good friends? Did she just hand me over and say, "Here I don't want her anymore. You can have her"? Why would my mom take me like that? Isn't it illegal? Did Rose sign papers so Mom could adopt me? What about my father? Didn't he have to sign me over too?* Feeling frustrated and a little sick to her stomach, she called out to God. "Why is it such a bad thing to want to know your true mother?" Tears started to fill her eyes when a still, small voice inside her heart asked, *what is a true mother?"*

I'm going to be one, she thought and realized it was more than just giving birth; it was in the love and care in the raising of the child, and that was what she had in her mom and dad back home.

"Oh, God, I'm so confused. Help me to appreciate what I have and stop feeling so thrown away." Jane arrived home just as the sky was darkening and was so pleased to see a light in the window. Matt was waiting up for her. How beautiful the house looked, so inviting. "Thank you, God, for my home and for getting me home safely." She parked the car and ran to the door.

Matt had been watching for her and flung the door wide, grabbing Jane in a big hug. "Oh, sweetheart, I'm so glad you're home."

"Matt, I've missed you so very much. Let's not be apart again," Jane murmured between kisses.

After a warm embrace, Matt went to get her bags, and Jane walked through the house, hugging herself.

He put her bags in the bedroom while she slipped into her PJs and robe.

"I'll unpack in the morning. I have so much to tell you. Mark told me that Rose had gone through all the tests possible because they wanted a baby, and she was incapable of pregnancy. She was not my birth mother."

"What?" Matt exclaimed. "You're kidding, right? But your mother told you her name was Rose, and even where she had moved to in Vermont. How can that be? If it wasn't Rose, then why did your mother tell you that?"

"I don't know. I'm going to visit Mom and see if I can get to the bottom of this, but first, I need a couple days to think it all over and decide how to approach Mom and Dad with this. Oh, Matt, since Mark told me about Rose, I've felt confused and unsure about everything except you, me, and our baby. I'll call Mom tomorrow and let her know I'm home and just a little tired. I'll tell her I need a few days to settle in, and then we'll visit. I need you with me, when I talk with her and Dad. I'm so afraid. What's going on?"

Matt put his arms around his wife and held her. "Sweetheart," he said, "I want you to rest and take it easy. I wish I could stay with you, but work calls. I'll try to be home early tomorrow and we can talk some more."

"I'm so upset, Matt. How could all this happen?"

"I don't know. It doesn't make sense, but we'll figure it all out in time. Now let's try to get some sleep."

Chapter Seven

Mark was very troubled. He knew what he said hurt Jane, but it was the truth. He yelled out, "I need to talk with you, Rose!" But of course she didn't answer; she would never answer. *It really isn't my problem,* he thought. *Forget it*. But he couldn't. It haunted him and gave him no rest. He had liked Jane and it was quite a story. *Who is this Paula and how did Rose come into all this? Lies were told, that was for sure but why? Let's see, what do I know, Paula and Rose were from California, someplace unknown as of yet. Who is this Paula? Why did she lie to her daughter?*

Why hadn't Rose ever talked about her days in California or about Paula? I thought she had just put California behind her, almost forgotten, as no longer part of her or her life. She had mentioned she was from there. Did she say where? I don't remember. We were so happy. This was our life, here on the farm.

I was in California years ago, he thought, *when I was shipping out with the navy from San Diego. I remember how sick I was. I hadn't enjoyed the crossing. The water was rough, seas running high. When I returned to the states it was to San Diego again where I mustered out of the navy. I remember spending a little time sightseeing before coming east. I had fun there and met some nice people. As a matter of fact, the night before I left to go overseas, I picked up this cute gal in a bar and had a good 'ole time with her. Boy was I hung over the next day when I boarded the ship. My stomach was already complaining. I promised myself never to get that drunk again.* He laughed at the memory of being so young and stupid. *What was her name anyway? I can't even remember what she had looked like. I remember she was celebrating her birthday and she and her friend had argued over her drinking too much.* He laughed, remembering how pissed she was at her friend. He had offered to buy her a drink, and they had hit it off right away. He was starting to remember now *a cute little thing with red hair. What was her name?* He tried to put his thoughts away and do some work in the garden, and it was okay for a while, but they kept coming back. *I wonder whatever happened to that cute girl, just turned eighteen, who I introduced to love.* Putting aside the memories wasn't easy, and that night dreams disturbed him again.

He awoke with a memory tugging at him, just out of reach. As he thought about things he realized that the connection was how Paula knew Rose. Thinking back on what Jane said about them, he tried to remember how they knew each other. *I don't think Jane knew either,* he thought. *Wow, so many lies here.*

Mark managed to get through the day somehow, even with the past tugging on him. *I don't have anything to do with their problem or their past, do I?* "What is it?" he asked himself. "Something is there. I have this feeling I know something."

It kept worrying him, and that night as he lay in the dark trying to remember, he dozed off and dreamed about the redhead in San Diego. She looked somehow familiar. *Who did she look like, a little like Rose but no,* then it came to him, the redhead, she looked like Jane. When he had first seen Jane it gave him a shock, but it wasn't Rose she looked like. It was ... "Oh no!" he yelled. Jumping out of bed, he tore to the mirror and looked at himself. "Dear God, could it be? Was her name Paula?" he questioned himself and honestly didn't remember. "What am I going to do?" he asked himself. It was just before he shipped out Rose and Paula in California, friends at the party that night. Mark's memory was coming back, and he felt sick. He had spent the night with Paula and never heard from her or saw her again. He could picture the two of them in his mind, Rose, the quiet one, who had argued with Paula and left early. He hadn't paid much attention to Rose. It was Paula whom he had flirted with, telling her he was shipping out and facing great danger, making her think of him as a warrior hero and hoping to get a night of pleasure before he left San Diego. Paula had been young, just eighteen, and celebrating her birthday, and Mark was ready and willing to help her have a good time. That couldn't possibly be the same Rose he had married, could it? No, he would surely have known. But then he only saw her for a short while. His attention had been on Paula, who was all over him.

Oh no, he thought. *Can it be? No way. No. Rose, Rose, is it true? Did you know? What shall I do?* Mark doubled over, groaning in pain. "Rose," he uttered, "Rose. Now calm down," he told himself. "This does not mean that this Paula had gotten pregnant by me, did it?" Had he used protection? "I don't remember," he cried out loud, talking to himself. The possibility that Jane might not be Rose's daughter but his daughter hit him. He was in deep despair and anguish, the pain unbearable, and he reached for the only comfort he knew. Jack Daniels. "I need a drink." And he kept drinking until he passed out on the couch, his senses finally numb, and his mind no longer tearing him apart with the possibility.

Mark awoke with a head the size of a basketball. He was still on the couch with the empty bottle on the floor beside him. He knew he had cried in the night, feeling so ashamed for what he had done. Paula had been just a sweet kid, and he had used her. Stumbling to unsteady feet, he groped his way to the aspirin bottle, and then started some coffee. After two cups, he made his way to the shower, letting the hot water flow over him, trying to wash some of the pain and shame away that he was feeling. Dressed in clean clothes, he returned to the kitchen, but the thought of food turned his stomach. He poured more coffee for himself and sat down at the table. Head in his hands, he felt so lost. The coffee and aspirins were starting to work, and he found he could think, which he sure didn't want to do. *What a mess this all is,* he thought. *How can I straighten this all out?* He could just forget it all and consider it a closed matter, refusing to ever think or talk about it again. *But then, what if Jane…* He groaned again, and a feeling of despair settled on him. He felt a longing for it all to be true but he also felt a sense of betrayal to his beloved Rose. Again, he questioned *did Rose know?* Did she recognize him as that sailor of long ago? No, he was sure she didn't. Rose was not devious; she would have said something if she remembered him at all, and Rose never knew about Jane and never would now. He rationalized that the night with Paula was before he and Rose ever really knew each other, and it was not a betrayal of Rose. In a way, he was glad she wasn't here to see all this happen. There was the problem at hand. What should he do? Mark lifted his chin and took a deep breath. He was basically an honest man and knew inside himself that this would have to be faced and worked though. The truth must be known for his and Jane's sake. Jane might be his daughter. That decision made, he knew he had to go to see Paula.

Mark searched his mind for where he had put the paper Jane had written her number on. He finally found it, and sure enough, her license information was also on it. He remembered writing it down, thinking he would check on its authenticity. He got out the maps and found where she was located, remembering she had said Paula lived five miles from her. Should he drive or fly? He could rent a car. Yes, that is what he would do. Get this matter to a head as soon as possible. It was eating him up. Mark called the airlines and got on a flight in two days. He also called a local hotel and reserved a room. Taking care of all the details, he felt better. His confusion was clearing, and his thinking straighter, but there was a sense of anger and strong determination growing inside him. He felt guilty and disgusted with himself. Paula had only been eighteen, what he had considered fair game. He also felt like he had betrayed Rose somehow. The thought that Paula was at fault was there also, that she had come on to him. After all, she knew he was a sailor looking for a night's fun. He did nothing wrong. So why did this hurt so much? "Rose, oh, Rose, forgive me." What if Jane were his daughter? Then it dawned on him. *She is pregnant; I could be a grandfather soon.* All he could think of now was another bottle of Jack Daniels, but no, he realized that had been a bad idea, and he wasn't going that way again.

Chapter Eight

It was the third day since Jane had arrived home. The first two days had passed quickly for Jane, and she had managed to get some rest. Sitting in the baby's room, rocking with her hands on her baby belly, she smiled and sang softly. The peace that she had felt in that lovely church when she felt her baby move returned to her. Jane and Matt had discussed everything and agreed something was very wrong. They called Jane's mother and set up a visit for the next Sunday after church services.

Mark had boarded the plane, which took him to New York City, and there, on to Elmira, New York, where he rented a car and drove to Watkins Glen. He then checked into the hotel, and looking in the local phone book, he found David Carlin's address. He asked directions at the desk.

Should he call first or just drop in on her? If he called, she might just hang up on him or possibly claim he had the wrong person. What a mess this could all be. No, he decided it would be better to just drop in. Would she even remember him? Would he recognize her? He didn't want to do this but knew he must. What about Jane, should he let her know he was in town to see her mother?

Remembering her pregnant state, he decided it might not be a good idea to let her know what he intended to do. Maybe this whole thing was a bad idea, and he should just go home. He longed for the comfort of being at home with his Rose, doing nothing more than sharing dinner at the fireside and laughing over some silly thing that had taken place. Mark realized he was feeling sorry for himself. He was suffering for his lustful behavior all those years ago. He hadn't thought of the night's pleasure as anything more than just that. After all, wasn't that just doing what a man does? He had been so young and so foolish. He felt shame for the things he had done. It was in his loving Rose that he learned about true love, faithfulness, and loyalty to one person. He had truly cherished her. His conscience was really giving him a difficult time. In a way, he was glad Rose was not here to witness his shame, and yes, that is what he felt, shame. Then what if Jane was his daughter? He spoke to himself, "Mark, quit stalling and just get it over with." *Wait a minute,* he thought. *What about Paula's husband? How would he like me showing up? I wonder how big he is and if he is a violent sort? Calm down* he told himself. *Didn't Jane tell you about how great her dad was and how loving? He had always known he wasn't her real father, and he did tell her it was only right she should know the truth.* "Okay, Mark," he said to himself. "Here you go."

He didn't have any trouble finding the house. The directions the desk clerk at the hotel gave him were easy to follow, and he was soon parking in front of Paula's house. All of a sudden, a feeling of anger was coming up in him. He wanted to let Paula know what he thought of her. She pulled a fast one on him, getting pregnant and never telling him all these years, what a waste. Rose might have accepted Jane, and they could have had the child they wanted. No, that didn't make sense. Mark took a deep breath. *Okay now, let's stay in control. I'm walking on eggshells here,* he reminded himself. *I may feel like blasting Paula, but why should Jane be hurt, especially in her condition?* He found himself at the door, counted to ten, and rang the bell. In a short while, this woman, vaguely familiar, had opened it and said, "Yes, can I help you?"

"Hello, Paula. I don't suppose you remember me. My name is Mark, and I was married to Rose Merryweather. I met the two of you years ago in San Diego, California, just before I shipped out with the navy. Jane has been to see me in Vermont."

Paula gasped, turned white as a sheet, and stumbled backward. She looked like she might faint, and for some reason, Mark felt a sense of satisfaction.

"We need to talk here and now or later when your husband is home. You choose."

Shc stood frozen and then finally said, "Come in, Mark. I'll put the coffee on first, if you don't mind. I certainly need a cup."

She led him to the kitchen and indicated he should sit down at the table while she started the coffee. No words were spoken between them until it was brewed and she had poured two mugs full and put the sugar and cream on the table. Then she sat down and took a couple of sips and said, "Okay, should I start or you?"

"I think you had better start, Paula, with the truth."

Paula took a sip of her coffee, as if to fortify herself, and began, "Mark, I had just turned eighteen, and I was determined to celebrate. I was not a drinker and quickly lost my inhibitions. Rose was telling me to slow down, so I told her to get lost. We argued, and she left. You were very handsome, Mark, and you seemed to like me a lot. The story you told me about being a hero and shipping out seemed so romantic to me. I don't have any excuse for what we did except to say at that time, I didn't think it was wrong. I was eighteen and could do what I wanted. I was frantic when I discovered I was pregnant. I thought, 'How can this have happened?' It was one time one night. I thought of trying to contact you, but I guess I knew it was just what people call a one-night stand, and you would most likely deny everything, and to be honest, I couldn't even remember your last name. I struggled with what to do and decided to have my baby. Why should my baby suffer because of my deed? I determined I would love my baby no matter what. Rose was a problem. I didn't want her to know, and then she told me about her job in Vermont. She was leaving, moving away. There was a job waiting for her. It was perfect. She would never find out about the baby. When Jane was born, I was so happy. She was beautiful. I worked as a waitress, and later on, there was a convention in town. This very nice-looking man sat at one of my tables, and he came back several times. We talked, and well, to make a long story short, we fell in love. I was terrified he would find out Jane was really my baby and think badly of me, so I told him she was Rose's. I said Rose had abandoned her and gone to Vermont. She didn't want the baby. I took her as my own, and later, David and I married. He never knew the truth about Jane. What are you going to do, Mark?"

"Well, first I'm going to talk with Jane. You had better tell your husband about all this, as he is going to find out, you know. I feel cheated, Paula, of a daughter, and now that I know I am her father—I am, aren't I?"

"Yes, Mark, you are."

"There was no other man, was there, Paula? Mark asked.

"No, no, please believe me. You are Jane's father."

Mark hesitated and then said, "I believe I am about to become a grandfather too. Paula blanched even whiter. "Yes," she said, "Jane is pregnant."

"I'm not going to walk away from this," Mark declared, "so you had better have that talk with your husband. Poor sap. He's in for a surprise. I'll get back to you in a couple days. Don't bother seeing me out. I remember where the door is."

Back at the hotel, Mark put a call in to Jane. Jane was very surprised to hear from Mark, and when she realized he was in town, a visit was set for that evening at Jane and Matt's place.

When David arrived home, he found his wife sitting at the kitchen table. She looked like she had been crying, and there was no supper ready.

"Honey, what's the matter? Are you all right?"

"Sit down, Dave. I have something to tell you."

He sat and reached for her hands, which he held. He could sense something terrible had happened. "It's not Jane, is it, honey? She is all right, isn't she? Is it the baby?"

"No, Dave. Jane, Matt, and the baby are fine. This is about me and what I've done. Please hear me through while I have the courage to tell you.

"Dave, when I met you, I had Jane with me. I told you she was Rose's baby and she had abandoned her with me. That wasn't the truth. Jane is my baby."

She lowered her eyes as shame washed over her. Dave look stunned, as if he hadn't really heard what she had just said.

"I met a sailor and spent a night with him one night, Dave, only one night. I was eighteen and thought I was all grown-up, and I felt like a woman. I wanted to be a woman. I never saw the sailor again, and he knew nothing about the baby. I was desperate and didn't know what to do. I decided I wanted my baby and I could never give her away. I would do all I had to. I would be a good mother. Rose was my friend. She had gotten a job in Vermont and was leaving. It was easy to say it was hers and she abandoned her with me. You're a religious man. You went to church every Sunday. Remember? You would take Jane and me with you. Why, you even prayed in the restaurant before you would eat. Our first date was Sunday church service, followed by lunch and a walk in the park. Your mother and father were strict and very upright. They scared me. You kept telling me how important going to church was and how your parents would never accept a wife for you who wasn't a Christian woman. I fell in love with you, honey, and I couldn't tell you the truth. I was afraid you wouldn't have anything to do with me."

Dave was sitting there, a deep frown now across his forehead, and his mouth looking tight.

"Dave, say something, please. Don't just sit there staring at me. I'm sorry, really, I am. Please, Dave, talk to me, say something."

When he finally spoke, he said, "You tricked me into marriage. I married a loose woman. How many other men have you been with? All these years we've been living together are a lie. How could you tell your own daughter she was not really your baby?"

"Please, Dave, don't," she begged, tears flowing down her cheeks.

He raised his voice. "Stop crying. You make me sick. Church is just another part of your pretense. You're nothing but a hypocrite. Does Jane know about this?"

"Don't say these things to me. I love you and always have. There has never been anyone else. Please believe me."

"Liar. There sure was someone else. Oh my, he would be Jane's real father. What have you done to me? Who is he, Paula? What has happened? He's here, isn't he? You've seen him, haven't you? Did you sleep with him again? I've got to get out of here."

"Please, don't go," she pleaded as she heard the door slam. Paula collapsed on the kitchen floor crying. "Oh, God, help us."

Mark arrived at Jane and Matt's without any problem. Jane introduced him to her husband, and they shook hands and sized each other up.

"Sit down, Mark. I made some iced tea, or would you prefer coffee?"

"Tea is fine, Jane. You are looking well, and it's good to see you again."

When they were all settled, Mark asked about Matt's business, and they talked general talk for a while, getting acquainted. Then Mark asked Matt if he could speak with him alone. Matt looked at Jane, and his eyebrows went up with a questioning look. Jane rose and said, "I've got some things I need to do in the nursery. Call me if you need me."

When they were alone, Matt said, "Okay, what's this all about?"

"I didn't want to startle Jane with what I have to say, her being pregnant and all. I have a story to tell you, and as Jane's husband, I will leave it with you to decide how to handle things. Matt, I was not raised in a church my folks were defiantly not religiously inclined, and neither was I. Mom and Dad had passed away, and I was at loose ends, so I joined the navy. I was preparing to ship out from California. It was my last night in town, and I decided to have a good time. I went to a place where I figured I could pick up some nice looker and have some fun. I did just that. The looker's name was Paula. She was with her friend Rose, and they argued, and Rose left, which was fine with me. I had Paula alone, and she was drinking and flirty. We spent the night together. I shipped out the next morning with a huge hangover. I never knew Paula was pregnant. I never saw her again until this morning. It seems impossible, but I didn't remember Paula or Rose until recently, and let me tell you, it came as quite a shock. After all, I had met Rose in Vermont and married her, never realizing she was the friend from way back then. Years later, after returning home to Vermont, finishing my education, and becoming a teacher at the local school, I had the good fortune of meeting a beautiful woman named Rose. We fell in love and married. My dear Rose passed away this year from cancer. Jane showed up on my doorstep shortly after, thinking Rose was her birth mother. I knew Rose couldn't be because of a physical condition she had that made it impossible for her to conceive a baby. She never had or could have had a baby. I honestly thought Jane was trying to pull a fast one on me. Somehow, for some reason, I couldn't figure it out, and I decided to play along until I knew what her game was. You know about the rest, except that I finally put the pieces together and realized who Paula was and the possibility that Jane was my daughter. I have been to see Paula, and she has confirmed that fact. I am Jane's father, and Paula is her mother. I didn't meet David, Paula's husband, but I told Paula she had better tell him all about this matter."

Matt was looking as white as Paula had been, and he sat, stunned.

After some time of silence, Mark arose and said, “I’ll leave, if you don’t mind. I am staying at the Holiday Hotel in town. Please contact me when you have decided what to do and how to handle this matter. I do not want to see Jane hurt, but she is my daughter and carrying my grandchild. Goodbye.” And he let himself out of the door.

Chapter Nine

Matt called up to Jane, "Honey, Mark has gone, and I have to run an errand. I'll be back as soon as I can."

"Okay, Matt," Jane called back. "I'm almost finished here. See you later."

Matt got into his car and started to drive. He needed time to think. Where could he go, and whom could he talk to? He had the urge to go see Paula and have a few words with her, but what if she hadn't talked with Dave yet? Oh my goodness, poor Dave. How would he handle all this? Above all else he knew, he needed to protect Jane. This would be a shock for her. How would she take it? "Oh, God," Matt muttered. "Please tell me, how shall I handle this?"

A small, quiet voice spoke into Matt's spirit. "Go see Pastor Luke." So that's where Matt went.

Arriving there, he saw David's car parked in front. *Uh-oh,* Matt thought. *David must have seen Paula should*

I go in or go back home? If I go back home, what will I say to Jane? I know God told me to come here to Pastor Luke, I guess I need to go in.

Matt parked and decided to stay in the car and pray first before he went in. "Dear God, I know that you are the Author, the Creator of all life. Jane would not be here if it was not your plan for her to be born. Father, we are all sinners, and sometimes we do things we should not, and then we must reap the consequences of our actions. Your Word tells us we reap what we sow, but you have made a way of escape from our sins through our Lord Jesus Christ if we will only believe, and Lord, I do believe. I trust you, God, to take care of us all in this situation. Jane is your child, for she believes in you and worships you. I do not believe you will allow the destruction of this family, but somehow, you will turn it to good. I come against the enemy, who would destroy us in the name of Jesus Christ, and I command him to take his hands off of us. I thank you and praise you for your covering and protection, my Lord and King. Paula and Mark must now face what they did before you and us. Father, please extend your grace to them and give them the strength they need to face this difficult time. Please bring peace and forgiveness into this situation. Thank you, God." Taking a deep breath, Tom left the car and went to the door of the parsonage.

Meanwhile, inside, David and Pastor Luke were deep into it. Matt quietly sat down in the living room and waited. David had shown up and vented on Pastor Luke all his disappointment and anger over Paula. He told Luke how he had called Paula a loose woman. How she had lied all these years and made a mockery out of their marriage and parenthood of Jane. He was full of bitterness and the sense of betrayal.

"I have always believed in God and his goodness, but Pastor, why would he allow this to happen to me? Have I done something horribly wrong that God feels the need to punish me? Why didn't Paula tell me the truth about Jane? Why did she trick me into marrying her and lie to me all these years?"

Luke let him rant and rave until he had worn himself out, then Luke asked, "David, when you met Paula and started to date her, was she a believer?"

"No, she wasn't. She had no knowledge of God and had never been inside a church. I took her to services and told her about God. My goodness, you'd have thought she would have told me then. I told her about Jesus Christ, who he was and why she needed him. I didn't propose to her until after she accepted Jesus as her Savior. I knew God did not want us to be unequally yoked with unbelievers. I had been praying for her to believe. I loved her so and wanted to marry her. I believed her that Jane was Rose's child. Was I ever played for a fool?"

"Dave, don't you know that you can't save anyone, not yourself or Paula? Telling Paula about Jesus and telling her she needs to accept him because of what you say is not, true salvation. Paula was in love with you. Is it not possible that she didn't really believe but said 'okay' to please you? You made it important that you wanted her to do that didn't you? Could it be you manipulated her into becoming a Christian so your parents would accept her?

Only God can save a person. He calls them to repentance and salvation through the cross of Jesus. Did you see any sign of repentance back then? Paula needs true salvation, and maybe it's happening now. Maybe God is working repentance in Paula and maybe in you too. Is it possible that your pride is hurt? Pride is a sin. Forgive me, Dave, but is it possible your parents were proud of their righteousness as good church members? Has Paula, over all the years of your marriage, given you any idea that she was not a faithful and loving wife to you?"

"No," David answered, "we have had a good marriage. But I feel betrayed. Why the lie? How can I trust her ever again? Our whole life together has been built on a lie."

Luke said, "Has God ever forgiven you and given you a second chance? She did not know God then and sinned. You were raised in church. Have you ever sinned? Were you not sinning then, manipulating Paula to do as you wanted to make it easy for your parents to approve of her? We all sin and fall short. What about pride? What does the Lord's Prayer, which you have prayed many times, say? Forgive me, as I forgive those who have trespassed against me. I have known you and your wife for some years and find you both to be good people, trying your best to follow Jesus Christ. I thank God for Paula, maybe now she and you can come to a true and honest walk of faith and overcome the past. The devil decided to have her, and he wants you too. Are you going to give the devil the victory? Again, I ask you, is it your pride that has been hurt, that you have been deceived?"

David broke down at this point and started to cry. "Oh, God, I'm so sorry. Please forgive me. You're right,

Pastor Luke. You see, Mom and Dad were strong church members, and I wasn't given any choice I just did what would make them proud of me, what they expected of me. I confess I wanted Paula, and I was determined to marry her, but I had to get past Mom and Dad's requirements. I have sinned in forcing Paula to do what I wanted without giving her the chance to hear from God for herself. All these years we have been very happy and strong members of the church, just like my parents were, but I see it was pride working in me, not love for Jesus Christ. It was making a proper appearance before them and the community a cultural lifestyle that had to be maintained. Oh, God, forgive me. I have been cold and prideful. It is my pride that has been injured, and I guess it sure needed to be. It is now broken before you, and so am I. Dear Jesus, I forgive my wife. I have always loved and desired her. Help us, Lord Jesus, to come to true faith. I surrender all to you, according to your will. Father, may it be done."

Luke prayed also and a peace fell upon them both. It was at this point Matt joined them. Luke said, "You have arrived at just the right moment." Turning to Dave, he said, "There is one person missing that needs to be here. Dave, Paula needs to be here."

After Dave left, Matt said, "What a mess. I am so concerned about Jane. You know she's pregnant, and I don't want her to get upset, but she will have to be told. Mark is her birth father, and he wants a relationship, if possible. Our baby will be his grandchild. He has no other children, and his wife, Rose, is dead. He has no one else in his family alive."

"Do you know if he knows the Lord?"

"Well, he sure didn't when he knew Paula. I think he was on the way while Rose was alive. He loved her very much, but when she died, he was very angry with God for not healing her. I think if he did believe, he doesn't anymore. Pastor Luke," Matt asked, how do I tell Jane?"

"What's the matter, Matt?" Luke said. "Don't you believe God has the power to protect Jane from harm and keep your baby safe? Is your faith so shallow as to put limits on what God can do? Is Jane so weak? Did she not travel to Vermont alone seeking truth? Why do you feel now she needs to be protected from it? God's Word says the truth will make us free. Take a few minutes and search your heart. I'll put more coffee on and be right back. I have a feeling it will be needed." Pastor Luke did put the coffee on, but he also slipped into his den and prayed for guidance.

Meanwhile, Matt was also praying for guidance. He did trust God, and with a deep breath said, "Okay, I surrender it all to you, Father God. You are Creator of my baby's life, and I accept from your hands your will and give it all unto you."

David later showed up with Paula, who was in tears. She looked awful, broken, and full of pain. Pastor Luke greeted her with a hug and said, "Sister Paula, God loves you."

"How could he, Pastor?" Paula was crying. "I have done a very bad thing. It was only because I thought David would have nothing to do with me if I told him the truth. Well, I was right. Now he hates me. It was only that one time, Pastor, and I am so ashamed. I was eighteen and stupid, and oh, God, I'm so sorry. I love

Jane with all my heart, and I didn't want to lose David. He took me to church, and I met his parents, who asked me right off if I knew God. They let me know Dave would never be involved with a non-Christian. What could I do? I said yes. I lied, and I went to church with David, and all these years, I have done what he wanted. Why is God punishing me now?"

"Paula, God isn't punishing you. He is working a miracle for you. After all these years, you and David have an honest marriage. David, talk to your wife."

Dave knelt beside her chair and said, "Honey, please forgive me. I said some nasty things to you that I didn't mean. You have been all I ever wanted in a wife. I know you have been faithful to me. I forgive you for the lie and realize it was your own fear of me not accepting you that caused you to cover up. Your sin is now exposed, but so is mine. I have been prideful and pompous. You didn't know God, and I thought I did, and we both sinned, for neither of us really knew God. I realize church membership does not mean you are saved. It is a covenant with Jesus Christ and a following in faith and trust in him. We need a personal relationship with Jesus Christ, and then we should follow his command, without forgetting to fellowship with other believers. I've had it backward and led you in the same mistake. Kneel down here with me, dear, and let us ask God's forgiveness together and his blessing on our marriage."

Luke said, "Come on, Matt. Let's get the coffee.

When they were in the kitchen, Luke turned to Matt and said, "Okay, it's your turn. Go get your Jane."

Chapter Ten

Matt arrived home and told Jane they were needed at the pastor's. "Why, Matt? What's going on?"

"Well, honey," he said, "your mother and father are there, and there is something we all need to discuss."

"You're making me nervous. Can't you tell me what it's about?"

"I'm sorry, Jane, but you must wait until we are there. Please, be patient. Everything is going to be fine. Tell me what you did in the nursery."

"Well, you know that rocking chair you put in the room for me? I sat there and worked some more on my knitting. I sang to myself lullabies that I could remember, just practicing, of course. I have heard it said that it's a good thing if you sing to your baby while he's still in the womb. I'm getting him used to my voice, and I think he can learn, even in the womb."

Matt smiled at her and asked, "Do you really think he can hear you?"

"Of course he can. Notice we keep saying *he.* What if the baby's a she?"

"He or she, it doesn't matter. We will love the little one, no matter what. You know, that's just it. We love our baby, even now, when we haven't seen him or her. Imagine how our hearts will feel when we can actually hold him or her in our arms. Makes you wonder how a mother could possibly give away her baby, doesn't it? Do you think your mother held you in her arms and said, "There's no way I will ever give you up, no matter what I have to do?"

"But, Matt, we know that my birth mother did just that, only it wasn't Rose. I feel like crying, and I don't know why."

Matt said, "We don't have the answers yet, Jane, but we will soon. Remember how much you love your unborn baby. How you would do almost anything to keep him."

They had arrived at Pastor Luke's, and Matt helped Jane out of the car. Jane was confused and feeling a little scared. She started thinking, *Jesus, help us.*

Pastor Luke, her mom, and her dad were seated at the kitchen table drinking coffee. She could tell her mom and dad had been crying, their eyes were red and puffy, but they were smiling broadly now and holding hands.

"Hi, everyone," Matt said while Jane hugged them all and said, "Mom, Dad, are you all right?"

"Almost," Paula said. "We just have a little more to make right. Sit down, honey, Matt."

Her mom began, "Jane, I am going to tell you something that is wonderful for me to finally be able to say to you, and yet, it is very hard to admit to you what I have done. I want you to remember that I love and have always loved you and your dad with all my heart. We are a family and a good one." Jane reached for Matt's hand and held on tight.

"When I was eighteen, I had never been in a church and knew nothing about Jesus. I just knew I was eighteen and grown and no one was going to tell me what to do anymore. I had a huge chip on my shoulder. I guess I was hungry for life but had little understanding of what true life was. I decided to celebrate my birthday in a way that I thought was grown-up and adult, as a woman of eighteen and on my own. I went to a club with Rose, my friend. There, we met a handsome sailor in uniform. I went crazy over him and flirted outrageously. He kept buying me drinks, and Rose and I got into an argument. I told her to get lost. She couldn't tell me what to do, and she could just mind her own business. Rose left and went home. I went with the sailor, and we ended up in his bed.

"The next morning he shipped out, and I went home with a hangover. Later, I found out I was pregnant. I couldn't even remember the sailor's name. I am ashamed of myself and what I did, but I do not regret it. There was no way to get in touch with him. Rose had been hired by a place in Vermont and was leaving. I never told her about the pregnancy. I decided that I would have my baby and keep her.

"I loved my baby from the first moment. I never ever thought of giving her up. She was mine, and I would do all I needed to keep her. I sought out some help from an unwed mothers group, and I finally gave birth to my daughter. She was so very beautiful. Just holding her in my arms made my heart ache with the depth of love I was feeling. I knew things would be tough, but I was willing to work hard and take care of us. After a while, I was able to get a job as a waitress, where I worked to provide for my baby and me. I took good care of my darling daughter.

"Then I met David." She reached toward him and took his hand again. "He was a good man, who took me to church and taught me about God. I learned that godly people don't have sex outside of marriage, that marriage is sacred and ordained by God. I couldn't tell your father the truth about my baby because I was in love with him, and I didn't want to lose him or have him think I was no good. I was not ashamed of the baby, just of myself. I didn't want to lose David, so I told him my daughter was really Rose's and she had abandoned her with me. Jane reached for her husband's hand and was holding on for dear life.

"Jane, darling, all these years, it's been killing me that you didn't know the truth. Jane, you are my baby girl, and I am your birth mother. When you told me you were going to Vermont to find Rose, I panicked. I only hoped she would turn you away, saying she didn't know what you were talking about, that you weren't hers. I thought somehow I could stall and you would, in time, forget all about finding your birth mother, being so busy having your own baby. I wanted to tell you the truth, but I was so afraid.

"That's not all." She took a deep breath, a swallow of coffee, and looked at her husband, who squeezed her hand in encouragement. "Honey, when you went to Vermont to see Rose, the man you found, Mark, was the sailor from so long ago. He is here in town. He came to see me. He had met Rose in Vermont, and they fell in love and married. Rose never knew about you or Mark and me. Mark had forgotten all about me and that night. Mark had forgotten all about the friend, Rose, from years before. She had made a life for herself in Vermont and then with Mark. She never mentioned her friend of long ago and probably had forgotten all about me. Jane, Mark is your birth father."

Jane sat, stunned. She was gripping Matt's hand so hard it hurt. The pastor was praying under his breath, and Paula was holding hers. David had his head down and was also praying for all he was worth. No one said anything for about five minutes or so. Then Paula, with tears running down her face, reached for Jane, honey, please forgive me. I'm so sorry, honey. I truly love you. I always have."

Pastor Luke set a glass of water in front of Jane, and she gratefully drank from it. She was still looking stunned. They waited.

Finally, when the tension had reached the breaking point, Jane took a deep breath and spoke. With tears running down her face but with a smile in spite of it, she said, "Dear Lord Jesus, thank you for the great blessing you have given me. This day, I have my miracle. This day, we all have our miracle. I have found my true mother, and I have found a true father in David. This is my family and has been since my birth. I love you, Mom and Dad, with all my heart. I am glad you told me the truth. Mom, God will honor that. We are all sinners, you know. That is why our dear Lord Jesus came to redeem us by his sacrifice on our behalf, so we could be reunited with our heavenly Father. God has also given to me this day a birth father. I will honor that, for I have come to know Mark and care about him. He will be my baby's grandfather, just as Dad, you will be. Matt, our son will have a special blessing in his grandparents. Mark's love for Rose was all he had. Now he has a daughter and a grandchild on the way. I have two families to love and for my baby to love. My cup runs over. Thank you, Lord."

Jane got up and, with tears running down her cheeks, hugged and kissed her dad and mom. Luke said, "Praise God, but there is still one more thing to be taken care of—Mark. You don't really need me for that. How about you take care of Mark and bring him with you to service Sunday? Perhaps the Lord will touch him and bring healing to his heart also." It was agreed, and with a prayer of thanksgiving to God for each other and for their very special pastor and his wisdom that God had given him, they said their goodbyes.

The next day, Matt called Mark and invited him for dinner. Paula and David showed up after the dinner had finished, and they told the story again, introducing Mark to his new family and letting him know how they saw him, as part of them and a member of the family. Mark felt a strange awe at finding Jane actually was his daughter and knowing the baby she carried would be his grandchild. He and Dave had a man-to-man talk outside on the back porch. Mark was amazed at the attitude of forgiveness Dave had for Paula and him. Mark understood the depth of true love, having loved his Rose. Dave told him how he had struggled with Paula's revelation but how the Holy Spirit had been with him and reminded him of what true love is like: Jesus Christ, who gave his life on the cross so man could know salvation from his sins and be reunited with the heavenly Father. God had forgiven Paula, and so could he.

"Mark, I forgive you for what happened between you and Paula. I was so stubborn and thought I was better than her. That made her feel she couldn't tell me the truth."

"I'm sorry, Dave, but you're right your attitude stunk and so did mine. I can hardly believe you could forgive me."

Dave looked at him thoughtfully and asked, "How about coming to church with us tomorrow? We are now fathers together of one beautiful daughter."

Mark went back to his hotel that night feeling very strange. His anger was gone, and he felt funny, somehow confused. He had a lot to think about. This was not what he had expected when he decided to face Paula, and he was surprised to find he liked Dave and Matt. They had told him he was now family. Is that what he wanted? How strange it felt to say, "My daughter, Jane." Could he just put all this aside and accept this new family? He fell asleep and dreamed of Rose smiling on him.

Chapter Eleven

What a glorious service they had Sunday morning. Pastor Luke preached about Jesus' work of salvation with anointed power. God's call was stirring in all the hearts of the congregation. Mark surrendered, and with tears in his eyes, went to the altar and gave his life over to Jesus as his Savior, Lord, Master, and King. His new family gathered around him in prayer. The glory of the Lord was all over them. A new soul came into the kingdom that day.

You see, there are two kingdoms. One is God's kingdom, meant for his children, who are the bride of Christ. The ones he calls and the ones who answer his call; the true believers who are in a relationship with their Lord Jesus Christ walk with him throughout their life on this earth and look forward to spending eternity with him. They are known as the bride of Christ, for they will be united with him forever. He calls them to the knowledge of the truth that he is the Savior of us all and gave his life on the cross to pay the price for our sin. We need only believe this in faith.

One is of this fallen world, which Satan rules. He has filled it with idols and destruction and every sort of evil. Many are those who succumb to his call, for hell is very hungry.

These are the mockers and liars and those who exalt themselves and live only for their own desires.

> Be self-controlled and alert. Your enemy the devil prowls around like a roaring lion looking for someone to devour.
>
> 1 Peter 5:8 (NIV)

Father God also calls us to enter into his kingdom. He gives us eternal life through his son, Jesus Christ.

> For God so loved the world that he gave his one and only Son, that whoever believes in him shall not perish but have eternal life. For God did not send his Son into the world to condemn the world, but to save the world through him. Whoever believes in him is not condemned, but whoever does not believe stands condemned already because he has not believed in the name of God's one and only Son.
>
> John 3:16–18 (NIV)

God is love and loves each and every person. He desires them in his kingdom with him, but he allows them to choose whom they will follow. The entrance into God's kingdom is through faith in the only true Savior, Jesus Christ, who died on the cross, shed his blood to pay the penalty for our sins, and rose from the dead, alive forevermore. He calls, "Come to me." Life on this earth is temporary, and there are sufferings and difficult times for everyone. God, as a loving Father, teaches his children through the Holy Spirit's presence with them, and he also tests their faith and trust of him. He is there throughout it all, and at the end of your earthly life, he takes you home to be with him.

For the first time since Rose's death, Mark was at peace. He sat on his porch with his grandson on his knee. "Davy," he says, "I want you to know your great-great-grandfather bought this land and started this farm, and it has passed down from generation to generation, your mother being the fourth and you are the fifth. I have prayed to our dear Father in heaven that you will have the joy of true salvation and of bringing forth the sixth."

Epilogue

That if you confess with your mouth Jesus is Lord, and believe in your heart that God raised him from the dead, you will be saved. For it is with your heart that you believe and are justified, and it is with your mouth that you confess and are saved. For the scripture says: Anyone who trusts in him will never be put to shame.

Romans 10:9–11 (NIV)